A DORLING KINDERSLEY BOOK

Senior Designer Claire Jones
Senior Editor Caryn Jenner
Editor Fiona Munro
Production Katy Holmes
Photography Dave King

First published in Great Britain in 1997
by Dorling Kindersley Limited,
9 Henrietta St, London WC2E 8PS

Visit us on the World Wide Web at: http://www.dk.com

A CIP catalogue record for this book is available at the British Library.

ISBN 0 7513 7061 4

Reproduced in Italy by G.R.B. Graphica, Verona
Printed and bound in Italy by L.E.G.O.

Acknowledgments
Dorling Kindersley would like the thank the following
manufacturers for permission to photograph copyright material:
Ty Inc. for "Toffee" the dog and "Freddie" the frog

Dorling Kindersley would also like to thank
Barbara Owen, Dave King and Kier Lusby
for their help with props and set design.

Can you find
the little bear
in each scene?

P.B. BEAR

Sandcastle Surprise

Lee Davis

DORLING KINDERSLEY

LONDON • NEW YORK • STUTTGART • MOSCOW

One hot summer's day, P.B. Bear and
his friends went to the seaside.
On the beach, they met Salty the seagull.
"Hello," said Salty. "I'm listening to the sea."
P.B. Bear, Florrie and Dermott listened.
SSSHHH, SSSHHH they heard
as the waves lapped onto the sand.

"Look at the big waves in the sea," said Salty. "I'm going for a ride on them." The waves rushed forwards, then rolled backwards. Salty bobbed up and down, up and down.

"Come on!" said Dermott. "Let's go paddling!" He splashed into the sea. SSSHHH, SSSHHH went the waves on the sand.

"I'm going to collect seashells," said Florrie. She set off along the beach with her basket and her bucket.

"I'm going to build a fantastic sandcastle," said P.B. "I'll build it right here."
He scooped up some sand with his spade and started filling his bucket.

Salty flew in from the sea and landed
on a rock near Florrie.
"I found a pretty shell for your collection,"
he said, and he dropped it into her bucket.
"Thank you, Salty!" she said. "Look, my bucket
is full of shells now. Let's go
and show them to P.B. Bear
and Dermott."

They saw Dermott splishing and sploshing in the sea.
"Hello, Dermott!" Florrie waved to him from the sand.
"Come and join me!" he called. "The water is wonderful!"
But Florrie saw a big wave heading towards Dermott.
SSSHHH, SSSHHH.
"Look out!" she shouted.
Salty flew towards Dermott.
"Be careful!" he cried.
It was too late.
The wave crashed on top of Dermott!

As the wave rolled back into the sea,
Dermott scampered onto the sand.
He was wet all over,
from the ends of his ears
to the tip of his tail.
"That was fun!" he said.
Then, with one big shake, he sent
drops of water flying everywhere.
Florrie and Salty laughed.
"Now we're getting wet, too!" said Florrie.
"Come on, let's go and see P.B.'s sandcastle."
Florrie and Dermott raced along the beach,
while Salty flew above them.

P.B. Bear saw his friends and waved.
"Look at my sandcastle!" he called to them.
SSSHHH, SSSHHH went the waves.
Just then, the sea rushed towards
P.B. Bear's sandcastle.
It came closer and closer.
"Stop!" he cried. "Don't hurt my sandcastle."

But the sea rushed onto the beach
and washed away the sandcastle.
"Oh, no!" cried P.B. Bear. "It's ruined!"
"We'll all help you build a new one," said Dermott.
"We can decorate it with our shells," added Florrie.
"I'll help, too," said Salty.
All of the friends worked together.

"This sandcastle is even better!"
said P.B. when they had finished.
"But sandcastles don't last forever," said Salty.
"Soon the waves will wash this one away, too."
SSSHHH, SSSHHH went the sea,
as it came closer and closer.
"Never mind," said P.B. Bear.
"Let the waves wash away our sandcastle.
We'll just build another one!"